HOT PACKAGE

A *HOSTILE OPERATIONS TEAM* CHRISTMAS NOVELLA

USA TODAY BESTSELLING AUTHOR

LYNN RAYE HARRIS

www.**lynnrayeharris**.com

Printed in the United States of America

First Edition: February 2014
Library of Congress Cataloging-in-Publication Data

Harris, Lynn Raye
Hot Package / Lynn Raye Harris. – 1st ed

ISBN-13: 978-0-9894512-8-4

1. Hot Package—Fiction. 2. Fiction—Romance
3. Fiction—Contemporary Romance

OTHER BOOKS IN THE *HOSTILE OPERATIONS TEAM* SERIES

Hot Pursuit (#1) – Matt and Evie

Hot Mess (#2) – Sam and Georgie

Hot Package (#3) – Billy and Olivia

Dangerously Hot (#4) – Kev and Lucky

COMING SOON:

Hot Shot (#5) – Jack and Gina

ONE

Two days before Christmas...

OLIVIA REESE WAS IN TROUBLE. Big trouble. And it had nothing to do with the fact it was nearly Christmas and she was spending it all alone. Unlike last year, when she'd been wrapped up in Billy "The Kid" Blake's arms. That was the first Christmas in a long time where she'd been happy and filled with thoughts of the future.

She pushed away memories of slick skin, hard muscles, and utter bliss, and pulled in a deep breath. Then she scrolled through the documents on her computer one more time. She'd been working for Titan Technology for the last few months, in their PR department, and she'd bought the company spiel—hook, line, and sinker. She'd seen the test results for their revolutionary weapons guidance system, and she'd put together the package to convince Congress why Titan should supply the next generation of targeting systems to the Army.

Her eyes blurred as she reread the results she was seeing onscreen—the *real* results. Everything she'd been told was a lie. Everything she'd believed and everything she'd worked to sell. She'd thought she was helping to protect men like Billy, warfighters who put their lives on the line for this country every day.

A chill went through her then, because if this sale went through, she'd be helping to dig their graves instead.

Olivia put her hand to her mouth and sat there with her heart in her throat, imagining Billy fighting in some war-torn country, depending on this equipment to save his life. And when it failed…

A noise in the outer office forced Olivia's head up. It was late and dark in the company's offices in Arlington, Virginia, but she'd stayed behind to catch up on some work after the Christmas party earlier that day. Tom Howard, the company president, had informed everyone they were to take the next week off in celebration of their certain victory when Congress reconvened in January.

They had the votes, according to him, and the deal was sewn up. The project was a success and everyone had been jubilant. There'd been champagne and much laughter. Olivia had joined in the fun, though she'd thought it was inviting bad luck even though Titan had outpaced all their competitors. Unless someone else invented a whole new system over the holidays, theirs was the best.

Except that it wasn't.

Olivia began to shake as voices filtered through the empty office. On instinct, she ejected the CD and stuffed it in her purse. It had come from Alan Cooper, Titan's head of development, and she still couldn't figure out why he'd sent her such a thing. Unless he hadn't meant to.

But it had been in a holey joe envelope in her inbox, clearly marked for her.

Olivia's belly churned as she ducked down behind her desk. She told herself it was silly to hide when she had every right to be there, but some little voice in the back of her head insisted. Two shadows moved past her office. She could see them flaring on her wall through the windows. She'd shut her office door, so unless they'd seen the light from her screen before she'd put the computer to sleep, they would have no idea she was here.

The time she'd spent with Billy hadn't been long in the scheme of things, but she'd learned a thing or two from him. And one of those seemed to be a healthy paranoia about people's motives and capabilities. She hunkered under her desk and waited for what seemed like hours. The office remained quiet and she finally came out, grabbed her purse and coat, and tiptoed to her door.

Olivia opened it quietly and listened, though it was hard as hell to hear anything over the pounding of her heart. She hurried through the office, keyed herself out of the security locks, and stepped into the outer lobby of the building that housed Titan Technology's offices. A security guard looked up from the desk and nodded at her.

"Ma'am," he said as she walked by. He called out again when she didn't stop.

Olivia spun around, her mind racing. "Yes?"

He pushed the book on the counter toward her. "You forgot to sign out, ma'am."

"Oh. Yes. Of course." Olivia marched over to the counter and signed her name on the appropriate line with trembling fingers. The guard checked the entry against her badge and then nodded.

Olivia hurried through the frosty parking lot. She got into her car, locked the doors, and glanced up at the windows to Titan's offices. Someone stood in the window, and she shuddered uncontrollably. It might be nothing. Probably was nothing. But if anyone wanted to know who had just left the building, all they had to do was check the logs.

It was starting to snow. Billy Blake listened to the excited chatter of the waitresses as he sat at the bar and nursed a beer. Two days until Christmas and it looked as if DC might get a white one after all. It didn't happen often, unlike back home. Billy thought of Sky Mountain, of his aunt and uncle's log cabin decorated for the holiday with twinkling white lights and a giant tree in the front window. His cousins would gather there on Christmas Eve and the whole family would drink hot chocolate, eat Aunt June's famous crispy goose, and sing carols around the piano until midnight when they would each open one present.

Then they would go to bed and arise much too early when one of Billy's nephews or nieces couldn't wait another minute to see what Santa had brought. Aunt June would fix French toast and coffee and the fun would begin again.

Billy wished like hell he could be there. But the Hostile Operations Team had an important mission coming up and there was no time to go home for the holiday. There hadn't been time for the past four years. Aunt June tried to hide her disappointment whenever she called to ask each year, but Billy knew. Aunt June was his mother's sister and she'd always treated him like her own. From five years of age, he had been. She and Uncle Jerry raised him when his mother dropped him off one day and never came back. He loved them both and missed them most of all at this time of year.

Billy shoved the beer away and tossed some bills on the bar. He'd thought he might like sitting in a noisy bar rather than in the quiet of his home where he could think about his family—or, worse, about the way he'd spent last Christmas lost in the delectable body of Olivia Reese—but he'd been wrong. He stood and shrugged into his jacket and walked outside. The snow was fat and soft and it was accumulating fast on the grass and the rounded lumps of vehicles. It was melting on the pavement for the moment, but that wouldn't last when the temperature dropped after midnight. If the Department of Transportation wasn't out with the salt trucks, this would be a helluva mess in the morning.

Billy wasn't afraid of a little snow driving. Growing up in Vermont, you learned real quick. But no one could drive on ice. It was best to stay home and wait for the thaw, or risk getting plowed over by some idiot who thought a four-wheel drive meant he could go where he wanted no matter the weather.

Billy dusted snow off the windshield of his Tahoe and climbed behind the wheel. It wasn't a long drive to the little house he'd rented but he was glad for the beast of a truck that would get him down the tiny lane. It still amazed him that you could be right here in the midst of a sprawling suburbia that stretched between DC and Baltimore, and yet still manage to turn down a road and find yourself in the country.

He liked that. He swung the Tahoe onto his road and flipped on the fog lights so he could see through the swirling snow. He'd gone about a mile when his headlights flashed on the shiny form of a car sitting sideways in the ditch. They'd taken the curve too fast, no doubt, and slid into the ditch before they could correct course.

Billy sighed and brought the Tahoe to a stop, grabbing a flashlight from the glove compartment before getting out and walking over to the car—a BMW 328i that still looked pretty new. There was no one in it so he went back to the truck and started down the road again. His headlights illuminated the dark form of someone walking up ahead. Hands shoved in pockets, hood up, head down, the person could have been a man or a woman if not for the skirt that ended a couple of inches above the back of the knee.

The woman wasn't doing a good job of walking, no doubt because she was wearing a pair of high heels. When she realized he was behind her, she tried to move faster. And then she stumbled off the road and down into a wide field that led nowhere. Billy shoved the truck into park and got out. The woman was trying to slide into the treeline at one side of the field.

"Hey," he called out. "You need some help?"

It was a stupid question, but he figured she was scared and didn't need him chasing after her. She stopped and turned and he spoke again as snow dissolved against his face and chilled his skin.

"Can I give you a ride somewhere, ma'am? Or you can use my phone to call for help if you prefer."

She began to move toward him then and he breathed a

sigh of relief. He hadn't really wanted to chase some strange woman into the trees, but he couldn't in all conscience have left her out here to freeze.

She had trouble moving up the slope and he went over to give her a hand. It was pretty dark, but her pale coat stood out like a beacon in the reflected light from the Tahoe. He gripped the flashlight in one fist but resisted the urge to shine it on her.

She grasped his hand with gloved fingers and he tugged her up the slope until she was on a level with him. She was shorter than he was—no surprise since he didn't encounter many women who were six-two—and small-boned. He looked down at her feet, wondering how on earth she'd managed to run toward the woods in those heels, and realized she'd lost the shoes. She was standing barefoot in the snow on a freezing Maryland road and that sound he heard was her teeth chattering.

Billy swore. On instinct, he swept her up into his arms as if she weighed next to nothing. She gasped and he opened his mouth to apologize for surprising her and to reassure her that he wouldn't hurt her.

But then she laughed and he stilled as that sound dove down beneath his skin and curled around his soul. He knew that laugh. Her hood had fallen back now and he peered down into a face he'd never thought he would see again. She'd ripped his guts out when she'd left. Not that he would ever let her know it.

"Olivia?" His voice was cold and distant. And filled with shock.

"Hey, B-billy," she said between chatters. "I w-was just c-coming to s-see you."

TWO

"YOU SHOULD HAVE CALLED FIRST." Billy stood next to a fireplace, poking the fire up higher, his face in profile to her as he worked. Olivia sat on his couch, wrapped in a blanket, a mug of hot coffee in her hands as she tried to thaw out.

"I didn't think you'd answer," she said softly. "Or maybe I thought you'd changed your number." Her teeth chattered on the last word, but she wasn't certain now whether it was adrenaline or cold. Probably both.

But she knew he hadn't changed his number. These days, with unlimited nationwide calling on cell phones, why would someone like him change a number when he was just as likely to move again in the near future?

Billy turned and sank down on a chair across from her—as far away as he could get, she supposed, without leaving his own house—and glared. Her heart turned over and she asked herself again why she'd come. Why she'd thought for one minute he could help her. This problem was bigger than he was. Way bigger. But she had nowhere else to turn.

She needed Billy's advice. But first she had to get through the pain of seeing him again, the sizzling attraction even now fizzing in her veins, and *think* about what had happened tonight.

"How did you find me?"

She didn't like admitting this part, but there was no getting around it. "A favor from a friend."

"A favor from a friend." He said it darkly and she swallowed. Special operators typically flew under the radar. Their real lives weren't necessarily cloaked in secrecy, but the HOT guys didn't exist in the real Army. If you wanted to find them, you had to know someone. And if he thought about it he'd know she could have only talked to a handful of people.

It had been sheer accident that she'd run across Matt Girard and Kevin MacDonald in the Pentagon one day a couple of months ago, but Matt had told her where Billy was living. He'd probably thought she might go see Billy, but she hadn't been able to do it. She'd held onto the knowledge of where he was like an old blanket she couldn't part with. She knew that all she had to do was find the courage to pick up the phone, or make a drive out to Maryland.

Of course she never had.

Billy scraped a hand through his dark hair and swore softly. "Never thought to see you again, Livvie. You made it pretty clear that was your wish."

He was the only man in the world who could call her Livvie and get away with it. The sound stroked down her skin like a caress, made her remember things she'd rather not.

"That wasn't my wish at all."

She'd been scared. And maybe a bit stupid. Not that she was telling him that, but she'd thought it often enough over the past few months. She'd rashly given him an ultimatum and all he'd said was that they needed to talk when he returned from the mission he'd been going on. He hadn't said he loved her and she knew he wouldn't choose her over HOT.

She hadn't said those words either, but she'd certainly felt them. She hadn't wanted to be the first to open her heart, but in that moment when he'd looked at her coolly and told her they would talk, she'd known what was coming. And since she knew what it was like to doggedly hang on to a man who didn't love you, she'd known what she had to do. She'd vowed long ago she would never beg a man for his heart.

Her flighty mother was still looking for love, still choosing the wrong man and hanging on tight until he dumped her and went for someone younger and prettier and less neurotic.

Olivia's insides twisted tight. Yes, she'd walked out on him. But he hadn't come looking for her either. He'd returned from his mission and she'd been gone. She'd taken the job with Titan and moved to DC. He'd never called her.

Billy's dark eyes bored into her and she knew he wasn't about to open up the Pandora's Box of emotion that lay between them ever again. So far as he was concerned, it was another mission; over and done and move on to the next one.

"You didn't come here to discuss the past. What gives?"

Olivia gulped down the acid rising in her throat. It

had seemed like a good idea to seek him out, but now she wasn't so sure. What if he told her to get out once she spilled her story? "I need your help, Billy."

His hot stare didn't waver. "My help."

She pulled the blanket tighter and swallowed. After she'd left the office, she'd been planning to go straight home and shut herself away for the night. Tomorrow, everything would make more sense. But as she'd pulled into the parking garage of her building, she'd felt the hair on the back of her neck start to crawl. It was probably nothing, but no way was she getting out of her car and walking over to the elevator knowing what she had in her purse.

"Someone sent me something and I'm not sure what to make of it."

He didn't say anything and she tumbled on nervously. "There were these files I shouldn't have seen."

Now his eyes gleamed with interest. If there was anything that lit Billy up like a Christmas tree, it was computers. And sex.

Jesus. Olivia closed her eyes and tried to shove away the image of a very naked and very hard Billy Blake hovering over her in that last thick moment before he plunged into her and rocked her world like no other man ever had before or since. Just last year, they'd been tangled together on the couch in front of the Christmas tree, nothing but the colored lights illuminating their skin as they made love. She hadn't put up a tree this year because she hadn't wanted to remember. Billy had the small tabletop tree from his aunt, she noticed, but it wasn't plugged in.

Though it probably had everything to do with her arriving unannounced and nothing to do with painful memories.

"Go on," he said.

"I work for Titan Technology now," she said, spilling the details of her job over the past few months. "We're about to get approval on a weapons guidance system for the Army."

Billy nodded. "Mendez has mentioned Titan. It's real revolutionary, what they're doing. It'll help a lot of our soldiers."

Olivia was sweating now. She pushed the blanket away and sucked in a breath as tears pressed the backs of her eyes. Dammit, she wasn't going to cry. She never cried. Not even when she'd told Billy to choose her or HOT and he'd chosen HOT. She'd watched him pack up his duffel, stared dry-eyed as he swung it over his shoulder and shot her a dark look.

"We'll talk when I get back."

But she'd known he'd made his choice. He'd walked out and she'd still not cried. She'd shook. She'd poured a shot of tequila. She'd watched a sappy movie on television and passed out after one too many shots. But she'd never cried.

"That's the thing," she said now, looking into the eyes of the only man she'd ever loved. "If what I saw is real, it won't help anyone. It's a lie, Billy. Nothing but a lie."

His jaw tightened. "You better tell me everything."

Since the minute he'd put her in the truck and brought her to his house, he'd been having a hell of a time concentrating on anything but the sight of her creamy skin. Her tights had been wet and ripped and she'd stripped them off in the bathroom before coming back out here in her skirt and turtleneck sweater. The sweater might cover her completely, but it was little better than the skirt because it emphasized the gorgeous curves of her full breasts.

Breasts he'd licked and sucked and touched many times in the six months they'd been together. His dick hardened as he remembered the way she'd writhed beneath him, her blonde hair spread over the pillow, her pink lips parting to gasp his name as he took her over the edge of pleasure and into something that had only existed between the two of them.

He'd fucked women before and since Olivia Reese, and none of them tangled him up inside the way she had. The way she still did. He was reeling as much from her presence as from the tale she told.

A tale that shocked and angered him the more she went on. She sat on his couch with her head bent and spun out a story that tightened his guts into knots. If Titan was falsifying their results in order to get a lucrative contract, then a lot of people could be hurt when the technology didn't deliver as planned.

"Someone sent you a disc," he stated, his voice as cool and emotionless as he could make it.

She looked up at him. "Yes. But I don't know if it was an accident or not."

"What did you do with it?"

"It's in my purse." She reached for the bag she'd set at her feet and dug out a CD-ROM.

Billy took it from her and grabbed one of his laptops from the desk. Then he inserted the disc and waited for it to open.

"Holy shit," he breathed when the information spilled across the screen.

"It's Alan Cooper's notes," she said. "He's the head of development for Titan."

Billy clicked another screen. "He has some screen shots here of test results. And then his notes that say the information was falsified."

Billy shoved a hand through his hair. It was pretty damning stuff. But there was no hard evidence here, just an engineer's notes. And without hard evidence, there was nothing to indicate this wasn't simply one disgruntled employee's attempt at giving the company a black eye.

"What are we going to do with it?" She sounded so hopeful, as if she trusted he had all the answers.

Billy sat back and blew out a breath. "Livvie, this isn't good enough."

She blinked at him, her green eyes wide and wounded. Dammit, he wanted to haul her into his arms and comfort her. *Not happening*.

"But those *are* Alan's notes. I don't doubt it. He has a certain shorthand he uses in his phrasing, and that's consistent."

"Doesn't matter. It's circumstantial. The screen shots are all for the results they've presented to Congress."

"So there's nothing we can do." There was an edge of anger to her voice.

"Not precisely. We need the real research, Liv."

"Then we need Alan. He'd know where to find it."

Billy turned back to the computer and clicked through

a few more screens. At the end of the last screen was a typed note. *Dig deeper. It's all there.*

He turned the computer and showed her the screen. She put a hand over her mouth. "My God. But why didn't he just copy the real information and send it to someone who could do something? Why me?"

Billy started to reach for her hand, thought better of it. What kind of brush fire would he be igniting if he touched her again?

"I imagine he couldn't get to the real information. Where is Alan Cooper right now, Liv?"

She blinked. "He went on vacation a couple of days ago. To St. Thomas."

"St. Thomas." Billy didn't believe it for a minute. "Who told you that?"

She hesitated for a long moment. Her voice, when she spoke, was a whisper. "Tom Howard." She bit her lip. "Oh God, Titan will be ruined if this goes public."

"Yeah."

"Do you think Tom…?"

Hell, he thought a lot of things. But nothing he was willing to speculate on just yet. Billy closed out the files and called up the internet. He'd hacked into a lot of networks in his life. It was his specialty on the team. Well, one of his specialties. They were all multi-talented in HOT.

"You got a VPN?"

Her forehead scrunched up. "A what?"

"Can you log into your email remotely?" Most companies needed their employees to be able to log into email from other locations in order to get stuff done, so they used a Virtual Private Network to do it. It extended the company's private network across the internet using gateways and kept it secure. *Mostly* secure, he amended.

"Yes."

He handed her the computer. "Here, try it."

She reached for the keyboard and typed in a web address and a remote login. Then she looked up at him. "I'm into my email. There's nothing unusual."

"Let me see what I can do."

She turned the computer back to him and he monkeyed around a bit with her account. He ran a few programs that allowed him access beyond her account, but there was nothing much to see. Titan Technology wasn't stupid and they had their important stuff locked away on a secure LAN.

"We'll need to go to your office and dig."

She swallowed. "All right," she said, getting to her feet with a resigned sigh.

He reached for her wrist, circling it with his fingers. He regretted it immediately. Her skin was hot and soft and his throat tightened. He let her go as if her touch stung.

"Not tonight. It's snowing too badly and your car's in a ditch. Not only that, but I need time to get credentials."

"Credentials?"

He gave her half a grin to cover his discomfort. "I assume there's security? A 24-hour guard and some sort of badging system?"

"Yes. During regular hours, we badge in and out. After hours, we have to sign the log as well."

"I'll need your badge to clone the RFID and to work up a passable duplicate with my information."

"I don't understand why."

"I have to hack the system… and it can only be done

from inside."

She looked grim. "My badge is in the car. When I slid off the road, I left everything but my phone and purse. I keep the badge in the door pocket so I don't accidentally forget it at home."

He stood. "Give me your keys and I'll go get it. Anything else you need while I'm out there?"

"Not unless you can find my shoes in the snow."

"Maybe. Doubt it though."

She folded her arms beneath her breasts. He tried damn hard to keep his eyes focused on her face rather than let them wander down over that tight sweater and every sweet curve she possessed.

She pushed past him and went to dig in the coat she'd set on a chair nearby. He couldn't help but let his gaze slide down to the rounded form of her ass. The red skirt she wore was every bit as tight as the sweater, hugging her hips and ass before ending about two inches above her knee.

She turned, her pale blonde hair swinging into her face as she did so. She'd gotten it cut since the last time he'd seen her, but he found that he liked it on her. It just touched her shoulders, so pale and silky that he wanted to shove his fingers in it and tilt her head back for old times' sake. And then he wanted to plunder her sweet soft mouth until she moaned and clutched his shoulders.

"Billy?"

He shook himself out of his reverie and stared at her hard. "Yeah?"

She came forward with the keys in her hand. "You seemed a million miles away there," she said softly. "Is everything okay?"

Hell no, it wasn't okay. Olivia Reese was standing in his living room, needing his help, and all he could think about was stripping her naked and losing himself in her body again. He didn't have time for this.

"Yeah, fine." He held his hand out so she could drop the keys inside without any finger brushing, but of course she set them in his hand gently, her fingers touching his palm and sending a lightning bolt of sensation sizzling through him.

He jerked his hand back and closed his fingers around the keys. "It'll take me about fifteen minutes, maybe more depending on the road."

"All right, but if you aren't back in half an hour, I'm coming after you."

His mouth twisted as he let his gaze slide to her feet. "Barefoot?"

"If I have to."

He recognized the stubborn tilt of her chin. "I'll be back. Don't run away, Olivia."

Her cheeks flooded with color and he knew he'd scored a direct hit. It didn't make him feel any better though. "Billy, I…"

He backed away and reached for his coat. "Forget it, sugar. I shouldn't have said that." He shrugged into his jacket and went over to the door. "Make yourself comfortable while I'm gone. There's some leftovers in the fridge, a few beers. Whatever you want, take it."

She stood there staring at him with those wounded eyes and her arms folded tight. He felt like an asshole. "Thanks," she said.

"You bet." He opened the door and slipped out into the frosty night. The snow was still coming down, a bit harder now, and he stood on the porch and breathed in the cold air, willing it to cool his temper and his libido both.

Since that was damn near impossible, he went and got into the Tahoe. Then he took out his phone and made a call. "Hey, Big Mac," he said when Kevin MacDonald answered. "Got a situation."

THREE

OLIVIA STOOD IN THE MIDDLE of Billy's living room with her arms still wrapped around her for a long minute after the door closed behind him. It was almost like déjà vu, watching him walk out the door. She shook her head and went into the kitchen to fix more coffee. Out of curiosity, she opened the fridge. Billy wasn't the typical bachelor in that he actually had food and not just pizza boxes. Not only that, but she knew he could cook a decent meal.

Something he'd learned from his Aunt June. Olivia sighed and pushed her hair behind her ears. She wasn't quite as cold as she'd been before, but she sure would love some pants—or at least another pair of tights—to keep her legs warm. And dammit, how was she going anywhere with no shoes? The pair she'd lost in the snow weren't expensive, but they'd been broken in and comfortable.

She knew that she couldn't fit into anything of Billy's. But she could wear his socks at least. She went down the hall, opening doors until she came to his bedroom. Even if it weren't the only bedroom, she'd know it was his by the duffel lying on the foot of the bed. She stared at the familiar sight and felt a pinch of something deep inside. Typically, the appearance of the duffel indicated an impending operation.

She closed her eyes, remembering how it had felt for him to kiss her goodbye and then not see him for weeks at a time. They'd only been together six months, but that six months had been punctuated by a lot of absences. She was familiar with the signs of departure.

She went into the room and opened drawers until she found his socks. Then she grabbed a pair of the thick socks he wore under his combat boots and tugged them on. They went halfway up her calf, and while she might look silly wearing them, she felt warmer already.

By the time she'd fixed the coffee, Billy was back. Snow glistened on his dark hair and eyelashes and his cheeks were red with the cold. He glanced down at her feet but didn't say a word. He tossed her badge on the coffee table—but no shoes—and took out his cell phone.

"Big Mac," he said after a moment, and she knew he was talking to Kevin MacDonald. "I've got the badge. Standard RFID. ... Yeah, shouldn't be too difficult to clone." He shoved a hand through his hair and stood quietly for a long moment. "Copy. See you in the morning, then."

He tossed the phone down and blew out a breath and she could tell that brilliant mind of his was working overtime. Warmth surged through her. He had every reason to despise her, but he wouldn't let that stand in the way of doing a job.

She curled her legs under her and sipped her coffee. "I really appreciate your help, Billy."

He stood there, so tall and hard and masculine. A lean

military machine just waiting for the go order. It made her shiver in a new way.

"And here I thought you hated what I did."

Heat crept into her cheeks. She'd known, hadn't she, that when she came to him, there were still things simmering between them?

"I don't."

"You tried to make me choose, Olivia."

She tilted her head back and looked up at him. "And I lost, didn't I? You didn't even have to think about it."

He didn't answer the question. "If you care about somebody, you don't put them in that position. You don't make them choose like that."

Her heart beat hard. "You don't get to say whether or not I cared about you. Only I get to say that. And I was scared of losing you."

"You wanted to control me."

She closed her eyes and pulled in a breath. "You won't ever see my side of it, so why are we going there? It's been over between us since you left for that last mission, and I know I'm to blame for it." Her eyes snapped open again. "But so are you, Billy Blake. It takes two to have a relationship. And you weren't ever going to give me more than a warm body in my bed for a few weeks at a time."

"We were together for six months. How in the hell do you know what I was going to give you if we'd been together longer? I said we'd talk, but you weren't there when I got back. You ran away, Olivia. Like a brat who didn't get her way."

She hated the way those words sounded on his lips, but how could she argue? She had run away. And part of her had regretted it since.

"I was leaving the Army and you knew it. What did you want me to do? Hang around and wait for you to come back every few weeks? I had resumes out, and you knew I could get picked up anywhere. But you never said a word about what came next. It was like you just thought I would be there, no matter what."

He glared daggers at her. "You were planning to leave the Army when we met. Why would I think you might need my input on a decision you'd already made?"

She gripped the mug tight. "Well, gee, I don't know, Billy. Maybe because I thought we had something but I wasn't ever really sure where you stood. You never said."

His hands clenched into fists at his side. "I kept coming back. To you, Olivia. I spent every day I had stateside with you. And that meant nothing to you."

"It did mean something. But I wasn't sure it meant anything to *you.*"

"Jesus." He shook his head. "Forget it. It's been too long and there's no sense raking over the past. You made your choice and we've both moved on."

Her eyes stung with frustrated tears. "Yes, we've moved on."

He turned away from her, all stiff military precision. "Good, great, end of story." He went over to the dining room table at one end of the long room and grabbed another computer. Then he powered it up and retrieved the disc Alan had sent her.

"What are you going to do?"

He sat on one of the chairs across from her. "Send it to HQ."

"What about security?" She knew he was a great

hacker, but there had to be others equally as good.

"This is a secure satellite link. Not a problem." He popped the disc in and his fingers flew over some keys. Then he sat back and waited for a few moments. When he was satisfied, he ejected the disc and closed the computer. "Mendez will get some engineers on this. Anything we can learn from here might help when we break into Titan tomorrow."

Olivia shivered. "I'm not breaking in. I work there." It was semantics, sure, but she didn't like to think in terms of doing anything wrong. It made it easier mentally.

"We'll start searching for Cooper too. If he's in St. Thomas, we'll get him."

"You don't think he is?"

Billy shrugged. "Honestly? I don't think so. But if we're lucky, whoever's behind the plot to sell faulty equipment to the military doesn't know either."

Olivia hated to think of what could happen to Alan Cooper. Or to her. "What if someone knows what he sent me?"

Billy's eyes darkened. "No one's getting to you."

"But going back there tomorrow..."

He lifted an eyebrow. "Who said you were going?"

"I assumed—"

He got to his feet now. "Hell no. You'll brief me on the layout, but you aren't going. It'll be me and one of the guys."

Anger flipped to life in her belly. "I realize this is what you do, but you won't get the information without me. Even with a fake badge and the codes, it won't work."

"Sweetheart, you'd be surprised about the places I get into."

"I'm sure you could tell me but then you'd have to kill me. But I'm telling *you*, Billy Blake, that you won't pull this off without me. Alan's office is in a secure area, and though you can hack into it, you need me—a recognizable employee—to watch your back. There won't be that many people working on Christmas Eve, but those that are there will know you don't belong. If you're with me, I can make it believable. Not only that, but if you look lost for even a second, you're toast. So face it, *sugar*, you need me to guide you and to watch your back."

Her pulse was pounding with adrenaline, both over standing up to Billy and over the idea she had to help him break into Alan's office. Yeah, there was a risk that someone knew Alan had sent her a disc. But that didn't mean they knew what was on it. Or even that it was potentially volatile. She'd been afraid to go home tonight, but she'd walk into Titan's offices tomorrow with a trained military fighting machine at her side. That was a no brainer.

Billy's jaw hardened. "I don't like it, but you have a point. We'll go in together—but only if my CO approves it."

She tilted her chin up. "He will."

"Don't be smug, Livvie."

She wanted to tell him she'd do whatever she damn well pleased. But the truth was that it was growing late and she was tired. There was no going home tonight, not with her car in a ditch and the roads snowed over.

"Look, I've been working long days and I'm tired. If you give me a pillow, I can sleep right here."

"You aren't sleeping here. You can have my bed."

She tried not to let her throat close up at the thought of sleeping in his bed. Surrounded by sheets that smelled like him. Oh God.

"You don't have to give up your bed for me. Besides, I fit on this couch better than you."

"I have a sleeping bag," he told her. "And I'm not arguing with you. Grab one of my T-shirts to sleep in. We'll hit Wal-Mart in the morning and pick up some jeans and shoes for you."

She got to her feet and stood there staring up at him. He was so close. For a moment she wanted to reach out and slide her fingers along his jaw. But she had no right. Not any longer.

Her gaze slid past him to the small Christmas tree sitting on a table near the window. He still hadn't plugged it in. She knew his aunt had sent it to him years ago when he'd first joined the military. Every year, without fail, he dragged it out. Because his aunt would ask and he wouldn't lie to her. He'd told Olivia that last year, the first and only Christmas they'd ever spent together.

"You're a good guy, Billy," she said, and meant it. And then she left him standing there and went down the hall to his room, closing the door softly behind her. She leaned her head against it and told herself it would be okay. Billy would help her out. And she wouldn't fall in love with him ever again.

FOUR

WHEN OLIVIA WOKE, IT WAS still dark. For a moment, she forgot where she was. But then it all came rushing back, along with the knowledge she was wrapped in Billy's sheets. She could smell him as if he were right here with her and it made her heart pinch tight with pain and regret.

She reached for her cell phone to check the time. It was three a.m. She groaned and then lay back and blinked up at the ceiling. It was Christmas Eve morning and a wave of loneliness engulfed her. She thought of her mother, no doubt drunk and in some strange man's bed right now. When she'd been a kid, her mother had dragged her from boyfriend's house to boyfriend's house. Only once had Olivia had a stable home life, but that lasted for three years before her mother chased Darrel Anderson away too. He'd been the most decent man Angie Reese had ever been with, but when he'd dared to suggest she needed to stop drinking and start being more of a mother for her kid, she'd had one of her predictable meltdowns.

Darrel tried to stick it out, but eventually he'd faded

away too. Olivia clutched the covers in her fists. She'd learned from an early age that men were unreliable, even though she knew that her mother was at fault too.

She knew it, but she'd never managed to convince herself to completely trust a man. Which was certainly why her relationship with Billy had broken down. She hadn't trusted that he would be there for her, and she'd forced the situation to a crisis.

Olivia threw the covers back and sat up. Yes, she'd forced the situation to a crisis and she'd lost. Best to know it sooner rather than later, right?

She slipped Billy's socks onto her bare feet and then ventured into the kitchen. Her stomach was growling because she'd failed to eat anything last night. If she could find a snack—some cheese, a banana, some crackers, whatever—she could go back to sleep.

Olivia halted in the door to the kitchen. Billy was sitting at the table with three computers open and that distant look in his eyes that he got whenever he was engrossed in some cyber puzzle. She cleared her throat and he looked up in surprise. And then his eyes narrowed as they dropped over her form.

She was wearing one of his T-shirts, his socks, and no bra. Or panties. Geez. She'd taken them off and washed them in the sink before hanging them near the heating vent to dry. Olivia crossed her arms over her chest and walked over to the fridge. The T-shirt covered her ass, but if she bent over or reached for something, it definitely wouldn't. Why hadn't she rummaged around for a pair of his sweat pants at least?

Because she hadn't expected him to be here. *Then why did you get his attention instead of turning around and going back to his room?*

"Sorry to interrupt," she said brightly. "I couldn't sleep and thought I'd get a snack."

He leaned back in the chair and stretched. His pectoral muscles bunched and flexed beneath his T-shirt and her mouth nearly went dry.

"You're not interrupting. I couldn't sleep either. Thought I'd go through some things."

She opened the fridge and found a package of mozzarella sticks. She grabbed two and turned around to lean against the counter and peel the plastic off the first one.

"Anything to do with Titan Technology?"

He looked at the computer again. "Yeah. Can't find a damn thing that indicates Alan Cooper left the CONUS for a trip to St. Thomas. Or anywhere else for that matter."

Her heart thumped. "Maybe he's hiding out somewhere." She hoped so anyway. She didn't know Alan well, but she liked him. He'd always been nice enough. Quiet, studious, a bit nerdy. A typical engineer.

"Could be. He's not using his credit cards, if so." Billy tapped something on the keyboard. "His last known location was a gas station in Alexandria two days ago. He filled up and bought a bag of chips and a bottle of water."

Olivia shook her head slowly. "I don't know how you do it, but I'm sure glad you're on the good guys' side. Think of all the mayhem you could do if you were willing to be bad."

He looked up, his eyes sparking with something that set up a thrumming deep inside her belly. "I'm willing to be bad," he said, his voice low and dark with promise. "As bad as you want me to be."

Oh God.

Olivia swallowed. Wetness flooded her sex, made her skin tingle with anticipation. She wanted him to touch her. Wanted to feel his body deep inside hers again, stroking into her so hard and fast that he made her cry out with pleasure.

Unfinished business. The words echoed in her brain, throbbed in her sex. How had she thought she could see him again and not be affected? She'd spent long days and nights remembering how it had been between them. She'd touched herself, stroked her body until she came, his name on her lips in the darkness of her lonely bed.

She'd had sex with other men. But she'd wanted Billy. Every time someone else touched her, she closed her eyes and pretended he was Billy. It hadn't happened often, but it was bad enough that she'd stopped dating altogether. One day, she could sleep with another man and not see Billy in her head, but that day hadn't arrived yet.

Not even a year had passed since she'd left him, and he still wasn't out of her system. If she pulled this T-shirt over her head now, how would she ever forget him?

"I, um…" Her skin prickled with heat. Her head swam. All she had to do was say she wanted him.

He got to his feet then and she could see the bulge of his erection straining against the cotton of his jeans. Her mouth went utterly dry.

He moved toward her. She thought he would touch her, thought he would take the decision out of her hands, but he reached past her and opened the fridge door. He pulled out a beer and went back to his chair and Olivia's heart thumped harder.

He twisted off the top and took a swig. "It's okay, Livvie. I shouldn't have said that." He pushed a hand through his hair as his gaze focused on the computer again. "I shouldn't have said a lot of things, but I find that I can't quite stop myself now that you're here."

She sucked in a breath and took another bite of the cheese. Disappointment swirled inside her. "Why is that?"

He looked up again, his dark gaze meeting hers. "Because I'm still pissed off at you. Because I cared about you and you left me without an explanation. And because, no matter how many women I've had since then, I still want to taste you one more time." He waved a hand at her. "Seeing you here in my clothes." He stopped. Swallowed. "Your nipples are hard, Livvie. And that makes me hard. Too fucking hard and nothing I can do about it."

"You've had *a lot* of women since me?" Her throat was tight. Out of everything he'd said, those were the words she'd focused on. And yes, her nipples were tight and achy and her body throbbed in spite of it all.

He didn't look apologetic. "A few. You?"

She lifted her chin. She didn't want to think of Billy with another woman. She knew he'd not been celibate, but still. "Women? No."

"You know that's not what I meant." He shook his head. "But damn if that doesn't make the situation worse. You, me, another hot blonde? Christ."

"I don't share," she said tightly. "And yes, I've been with a few men."

He slapped the lid of the nearest computer closed and shot to his feet with a growl. And then he was standing on the other side of the kitchen, taking another swallow of beer, and glaring at her. "Define a few."

Her heart was racing hard and fast and a current of something that could only be called joy was beginning to bubble in her veins. He was jealous. It made her heart sing even though it shouldn't. She should weep with all she'd lost, but instead she was standing here and feeling so many wild things bubbling inside her. Reckless things.

"Why should I? Are you planning to tell me how many women you've been with? Besides, we're not together anymore. It doesn't matter."

He glared for a long minute. And then he pointed at her. "You were mine, Olivia. I wasn't ready to give that up, but you made the decision for us both. So yeah, I'm fucking pissed that you've been with anyone else."

"Hypocrite." She said it softly, but he heard it.

His nostrils flared. "Maybe so but it doesn't change a thing." He stood there across from her, his body coiled and tense. And then he shook his head. "You better run, Liv. Get back to bed, and lock the door while you're at it. Because I've got a burning need to prove you made a huge fucking mistake when you walked out."

Her heart thudded against her ribs at the violence in his voice and the fire in his eyes. He wouldn't hurt her, she knew that. But he wouldn't hesitate to employ a little sensual torture. Not whips or chains or anything like that. No, he had a far more deadly weapon: his knowledge of her body and how to withhold pleasure for as long as possible.

Olivia shivered as she stared at him. He could make her warm again. He could make her hot, for God's sake. But how would that fix anything?

"I already know we had great sex, Billy. But sometimes that's not enough."

"Goddamn," he said softly. "You really don't get it, do you?"

FIVE

SHE STOOD IN HIS KITCHEN in nothing but a shirt that hung to mid-thigh and would show her ass if she lifted her arms. Her damn nipples budded tight against the fabric, her wheat-blonde hair gleamed in the overhead light like reflected gold, and it took everything he had in him not to walk over and rip the shirt over her head.

She was looking at him now with wide, shining eyes, and the beast tethered inside him roared to life. He'd revealed too much, but seeing her again had ripped open old wounds he'd thought were healing. She'd left him. She'd been in his life for months, in his bed, and though he knew she had issues with what he did, he'd never thought she would demand he give it up for her.

The bitch of it was, he might have done so. He'd been pissed, but then he'd considered it during the long, lonely nights out in the field and he'd thought *yeah, I could go for a regular nine-to-five at a company.*

He had a skill that translated well to the outside. And he'd had Olivia.

Or so he thought.

But she'd been gone when he came back, and all the anger and hurt of a lifetime had welled to the surface. His mother left when he was a kid and she'd never come back. That didn't usually bother him because he had Aunt June and Uncle Jerry and all his cousins. But sometimes he thought about it. About why he hadn't been enough for her. About why Aunt June would do anything for him while his own mother wouldn't.

"What are you saying?" Olivia asked, her voice small and tight. She'd wrapped her arms around herself, but it didn't help one bit because her breasts swelled against the shirt and the hem lifted just enough that he could see the shadow of her pubis.

She wasn't wearing panties. Billy's cock jerked against his jeans and he swallowed hard. Yeah, he'd been with other women, but it had been a while. He'd been too busy lately, and too uninterested. That last had begun to bother him recently, but he figured it was temporary. They were working pretty hard at HOT HQ in preparation for this operation in Qu'rim. Al Ahmad was there, hiding out and arming the rebels in the civil war against the king. And Lucky San Ramos, their dead teammate's widow, was the only person who could ID the terrorist.

Lucky wasn't happy about it, but she was here and training hard for the mission. They were all training hard. They owed it to Marco San Ramos and Jim Matuzaki to get this guy. Those two had died months ago now, on that fucked up mission to capture Al Ahmad's second-in-command. Billy had wanted to lose himself in Olivia's arms when he'd gotten home, but she hadn't been there.

Billy turned away and finished the beer. Then he set the bottle on the counter very carefully. "Nothing, Livvie.

Go to bed. Forget I said anything."

She didn't move for a long moment. But when she did, she didn't leave the room. She moved toward him, until he could smell her sweet scent wrapping around his senses. He stood very still and kept his gaze on the bottle rather than on her.

"What's wrong, Billy?"

Her voice was soft and sweet and he wanted to turn and tug her into his arms, bury his face in her hair like he used to do. What was it about this one woman that turned him inside out? He'd tried to drive her from his mind with sex and booze and hard work, but she'd never really gone away.

On some level, he knew that was pretty significant. But she'd run away from him, left him behind. If she could do that, then she wasn't as into him as he'd been into her. He got the hint and he'd moved on.

But here she was, in his house, and all he wanted was to strip her and remind her of how it used to be. Remind himself, too, because there'd been a sweetness with her he'd never felt before or since.

"Too much on my mind, not enough sleep," he said. "Just go back to bed."

She moved, but not away from him. Her hand settled on his arm, her fingers burning into him where they touched. She'd always had the power to set him on fire. It hadn't changed. He stood stiffly and waited for her to do or say whatever she was going to.

"I want to know what you meant. What don't I get?"

He met her gaze head on. She wouldn't give up unless he told her. So he would, and if it hurt her, then it was nothing less than she deserved. Because she'd hurt him.

"It was more than sex, Liv, and you know it. We had something special, but you threw it away. And for what? Do you even know?"

Her throat worked. And then her gaze dropped and he found himself looking at the top of her bowed head. He'd wanted to hurt her, and now he didn't. He wanted to hold her.

"I was scared."

He put his finger under her chin and forced her to look at him. Her eyes shone with moisture. "Of what? Of me?"

"Yes." She put her fingers around his wrist, held on. "Because you made me feel too much and I didn't know how to handle it."

"So you chose to run away instead of face your fear."

She closed her eyes. "I know that's not something you would ever do, but yes, that's exactly what I did. I'm not like you, Billy. I'm not tough and brave and willing to fight. I like to cut my losses, protect myself."

He just felt weary now. Weary and heartsick and angry deep down. Because she hadn't believed in him. In them. She'd run away, and she'd kept running until she needed something from him. Until she needed his help.

She'd come back because she was scared, not because she missed what they had together.

"One of these days, you're going to have to learn to stop running." He slid his fingers along her jaw, down her throat. He stopped just shy of ghosting them over her nipples, though he knew she wouldn't stop him. He dropped his hands to his sides. His cock ached, but it wasn't the first time. He could deal with it.

"I know. I'm trying." She slicked her tongue over her

lower lip and he just barely kept from groaning. If she touched him, if she reached out and put her hand on his chest, he was a goner. "Good night, Billy. Thanks for the food."

"Sure thing, Liv."

She stepped away from him and disappeared through the door to the hall. Billy closed his eyes. Then he went and got another beer from the fridge.

Wal-Mart was a madhouse on Christmas Eve, but they stopped anyway and managed to pick up a pair of jeans, a sweater, and some boots for Olivia. She was much warmer than she'd been last night when she'd been trudging down the road toward Billy's place. The snow had continued all night and there were big drifts of it on the sides of the roads where the plows had come through.

The roads had been salted and were passable, if not completely safe. But Olivia didn't fear with Billy Blake behind the wheel. He'd grown up in snowy Vermont, unlike her, who'd grown up in various towns across the south. From Florida to Texas and back again, she'd lived in every state that had once been a part of the confederacy. Snow was not a typical occurrence in her childhood.

She'd frowned when they'd passed her Beemer in the ditch, but Billy told her not to worry. The ditch wasn't deep, thankfully, and he'd promised he'd tow it out for her later when they finished their errand at Titan Technology.

Olivia hugged her arms around herself as they drove into the city. There was still plenty of traffic in DC, though not as much as there might have been if not for the snow and it being Christmas Eve. Behind them Nick Brandon, Ryan Gordon, Chase Daniels, and Sam McKnight followed in an unmarked communications van. She'd thought that many guys were overkill, but HOT didn't do anything by half measures.

They would've probably had the whole team along, except that Kev MacDonald was assigned to twenty-four-seven duty guarding Lucky San Ramos—and Jack Hunter, the sniper, was busy elsewhere. Not that they needed a sniper today. Or so she hoped anyway.

Matt Girard was back at HQ, directing operations. Occasionally Billy answered a call from him, but she never could glean what they were talking about. It was all code and shorthand and Olivia leaned back against the seat and closed her eyes.

She hadn't slept well. After that three a.m. encounter with Billy, she'd been unable to settle down. She kept thinking about what he'd said, about how they'd had something special but *she'd* been the one to throw it away.

Well, hadn't she? Olivia wanted to deny it, but she couldn't. On the other hand, how was she supposed to know what his feelings had been? He'd never told her.

But he'd also spent all his time with her when he wasn't in the field. They'd lived together without actually living together. He'd kept an apartment of his own, but he'd never stayed there. He'd stayed with her.

"Not many cars here," Billy said, cutting into her thoughts. She opened her eyes as they pulled into the parking lot. No, there weren't many cars, but there were always people who worked even when they could take the day off. "What about Howard's?"

She scanned the lot for Tom Howard's Jaguar. It wasn't there and she breathed a sigh of relief. "Not here."

Getting Billy inside wasn't going to be difficult, but if Tom were around, it would be a lot more challenging. They often had visitors from sub-contractors of Titan, from the halls of Congress, from different military branches—but Tom was the CEO and would know better than anyone what was expected and what was unusual.

Olivia breathed out a shaky sigh as Billy parked and opened the door. She joined him, her badge hanging on a lanyard around her neck and tucked inside her jacket, and they began walking toward the building. The van with the rest of the team was nowhere to be seen and she knew they must have parked down the street. They were in contact with Billy through a tiny ear mic, but that was it.

They walked right up to the door and Olivia badged in. Billy swiped his badge right behind hers because the guard would note how many people were entering against how many badges had been swiped.

"Hello, Miss Reese," the uniformed woman behind the desk said when they stepped inside. "Didn't expect to see you today."

Olivia smiled. "I didn't expect to be here," she replied. "But Mr. Blake needs to work on some software updates for the company Intranet. Shouldn't take long."

She signed into the log, making small talk with the guard about her kids and family plans for tomorrow. The woman turned the log and checked the entries against their badges.

"Go on in, Miss Reese, Mr. Blake. And you have a

Merry Christmas if I don't see you again."

"Thanks, you too."

Billy turned to her once they were in the elevator. "Doing great, Livvie."

She rubbed her arms through her coat. "Thanks." She would have loved to say more, but she was just paranoid enough to think that the elevator was wired for sound and the guard was listening in downstairs.

The doors slid open to the main floor of Titan Technology's offices. The lights were on and a couple of people tapped away at desks in their cubicles. It almost made her sad, in a way. What kind of home life did you have to have to be here on Christmas Eve, in your cubicle, when you could be watching Christmas movies or just taking it easy?

Then again, who was she to judge? She didn't exactly have anyone waiting at home for her, did she? She didn't even have a tree this year. She'd been planning to watch romantic comedies all night and then get together with a couple of single girlfriends tomorrow for dinner.

Olivia led Billy down the hallway, past her office, and toward the secure research wing where Alan Cooper's office was located. There was a cipher lock there and she didn't know the code. During work hours, if anyone needed in who didn't have the code, they called the secretary who sat just inside the door and informed her about their business.

Olivia glanced over her shoulder worriedly as they approached, hoping nobody was watching. The corridor was empty. The security cameras that normally pointed at the door were still there and her heart skipped. But the guys in the van were supposed to hack in and override the cameras, so unless Billy told her to stop, she figured it had been done and they were looping an empty hall.

When she reached the door, she stepped aside to let Billy get to the cipher.

He shot her a grin that said he was having more fun than she could imagine. And then he leaned forward and kissed her swiftly. It wasn't anything more than a kiss for luck, but her whole body ignited as if he'd swept his tongue into her mouth and squeezed her ass.

"Show time, Liv."

SIX

OLIVIA'S HEART BEAT HARD THE whole time Billy was at the keypad. But it took him less than a minute to crack the code. Her jaw dropped as he yanked the secure door open and motioned for her to enter.

She led him through the warren to Alan's office. It was locked too, but he had it open in less than a second. He stuck a long probe in the slot, slapped the end of it, and the door opened on silent hinges.

She closed the door behind her as he went over to the desk and powered up the computer. Her pulse raced and her stomach clenched, but she told herself that Billy knew what he was doing. And HOT was watching the cameras. They'd have advance warning before anyone else entered the building.

The six people already inside weren't authorized to enter the research area, so she had no fear one of them would stumble in. Still, her nerves were strung tight and her belly roiled with acid.

She let her gaze rove freely over the man at the desk. He was engrossed in his task, his fingers flying over the keyboard, his face lit by the screen. She loved looking at him. He was clean and beautiful at the moment, but she imagined he often did this with greasepaint and dark clothes.

The microphone in his ear was hidden, but he kept up a running commentary to the men at the other end. His voice was deep and velvety and she remembered him whispering hot words in her ear when he was buried inside her.

Geez, Liv, wrong time to be thinking about this.

But she couldn't help it. Not after last night and how close she'd been to throwing herself in his arms and begging him to make love to her again. She'd been aroused, he'd been hard, and there'd been nothing to stop them.

Nothing but tangled emotion and a deep uncertainty about what it would do to her to open herself up like that again. Could she have sex with him and not be affected by it?

Somehow, she doubted it.

"There's nothing here, Knight Rider," Billy said softly, his voice edged with frustration. Olivia didn't say anything because she knew he wasn't talking for her benefit, but her stomach fell into her toes.

"Not even his notes. Either Cooper's been very careful or someone's deleted the evidence."

He tapped a few more keys and gritted his teeth together. "Yeah, copy," he said at the same time the screen went black and he got to his feet. He was moving toward her before she could process that he was finished here.

"That's it? We're done?"

His face was grim. "We're done. There's nothing on the LAN but the official stuff. If it was here, it's gone now."

She told herself not to panic. "So what do we do?"

He stopped in front of her, his big form shadowing hers. She could feel his heat, his vibrancy. In spite of everything, she wanted to lift her mouth to his and feel his lips again.

"We have to find Cooper. He's the key to everything."

"How do we do that?"

He didn't answer. Instead, his head snapped up and he swore. "Copy," he said. And then he grabbed her arm and hustled her out of Alan's office and back toward the secure door.

"What's wrong?"

His mouth was a hard line. "Tom Howard's on his way up."

Olivia's belly took a nosedive into the floor.

"It's all right," Billy said. "We have a story, remember?"

"Yes."

She swallowed as they hurried down the corridor. The secure door was in front of them, the steel mesh window looking out on an empty hallway. If they could just get there and get back through…

"And what is it?" Billy said, interrupting her thoughts.

"You're from the Pentagon. A last minute operational check of our software."

"That's right." He sounded so smooth and calm that her heart slowed a fraction. They reached the door and Billy looked out. And then he opened it and they were through, heading toward her office. They reached it as the elevator dinged. Olivia gripped the knob with trembling fingers and twisted.

She could hear Tom calling out to Bob Jenkins, one of the guys in the cubicle near the elevator. And then he was whistling, coming down the hallway that passed in front of her office.

She sat at her desk and called up her email. Billy stood nearby with his arms folded and a stern look on his face. Olivia clenched her teeth as Tom got closer.

And then he stopped in front of her open door, his gaze darting from her to Billy and back again.

"Olivia," he said. "Saw you'd come in today. Everything okay?"

She pasted on a smile and stood. "Yes sir. Just showing the guy from the Pentagon a few things. He's doing a software check."

Tom was frowning. "I didn't realize we had anyone coming over from the Pentagon."

Billy stepped forward and held out his hand. He looked big and imposing in his jeans and dark T-shirt. He'd taken his leather jacket off and draped it over a chair and his bare arms flexed in a smooth ripple of mouth-watering muscle.

"William Blake, sir." He held out a card and Tom took it. "Colonel John Mendez sent me over for a quick check of a few things. You know the Pentagon." He crossed his arms over his impressive chest and stood there like a block of stone. And then he smiled as much as a military machine might smile. "We're real impressed with your product, sir. Can't wait to put it in the field."

Tom's face split in a wide grin. "Thank you, uh, Mr. Blake. We're very honored to do our part for our military.

You active duty?"

"I am not at liberty to say, sir. You understand."

Tom nodded. "Oh yeah, did a few years myself. Know all about those special duty assignments."

"Yes sir." They talked a few more moments and then Billy nodded at the card in Tom's hand. "Give the Colonel a call, sir. He'd love to hear from you."

Tom tucked the card in his jacket. "I'll do that, *Mister* Blake." He nodded at Olivia. "All right then, I'll let you get back to it. Merry Christmas, folks."

"Merry Christmas, sir," Billy said as Tom walked out and went whistling down the hall toward his office.

Olivia sat there blinking, her fingers hovering over the keyboard, her entire body humming with adrenaline.

"Log off, Liv," Billy said quietly. "Time to go."

Olivia did as he said, her heart thundering, ears straining to hear if Tom Howard was coming back, if he'd decided something was fishy after all. But Tom didn't come back and they were soon walking out the front door and climbing inside Billy's truck. He started the engine and sat there with his hands on the wheel, lost in thought.

"Aren't you worried he'll be suspicious?" Olivia asked when the silence stretched out.

He turned to look at her. "I expect he will be. But he'll call Mendez and Mendez will back the story up. Howard's the kind of guy who's impressed with the Pentagon and top-secret projects. He'll be satisfied."

Tom turned the card William Blake had given him over and over in his hand. Tom could spot a soldier a mile away, and that one was Special Forces if he was anything. His hair wasn't high and tight, but his manner and bearing said he was in the military and that he was elite.

Tom had been in the Army, but he'd never made the cut for the elite units. He'd tried, but apparently drill instructors weren't amused by brains. Yeah, he'd stopped to sleep for a few minutes when he was supposed to be humping to the next checkpoint, but he'd been so clever about it. He'd used initiative, by God, but that wasn't an acceptable excuse to a DI. He'd been saving himself, conserving energy, but the Army didn't see it that way when they'd caught him leaned up against the tree and catching a few winks.

He'd been sent back to his regular unit and that was the end of that. He hadn't re-upped. He'd gotten out instead, determined to make something of his brains and initiative.

And here he was thirty years later, about to be a very rich man. If he'd stayed in the Army, he'd be an order-following ground-pounder like Blake. Far better to be on this end of things.

Except, of course, when something went wrong. Tom flipped on the lights in his office and logged onto his computer, his heart suddenly pounding. Why was Blake here? Why did the Army want a software check on Christmas Eve?

He held his breath while he searched for the files. And then he let it out when he confirmed they were definitely gone. He'd erased them himself. Unless Alan had made copies, the evidence didn't exist. The technology would be deployed and it would work. Mostly. Regrettable when it didn't, but Titan Technology would fix that in subsequent updates.

And he would get very rich while they did. Yes, far better to use one's initiative.

"Sir?"

Tom looked up to find Tiffany, his very cute secretary, standing in the door. "I thought I gave you the day off," he said pleasantly.

"You did, sir," she replied with a smile. "But I forgot my allergy meds yesterday when I left so I came back for them. And I meant to tell you something yesterday too, but the champagne went to my head and I totally forgot."

She looked apologetic so he smiled in encouragement. "What is it, Tiffany?"

"You asked me to see if Alan Cooper sent anything to anyone before he left. And he did, sir. He sent a CD to Olivia Reese. The mailroom confirmed it just yesterday."

Tom's blood ran cold and his brain scrambled over every second of the interaction with Olivia and the military guy. Had she seemed nervous? Suspicious? Guilty?

He hadn't paid her much attention once Blake started talking. And maybe that had been the plan all along. His stomach twisted but he told himself not to get worked up. He hadn't gotten this far by being scared of a little bump in the road, had he?

"Thank you, Tiffany. I appreciate it."

"You're welcome, sir. Have a Merry Christmas!"

"You too. And please close the door behind you," he added, smiling as she did just that. And then he picked up the phone and dialed the one person who had more to lose than he did.

"This better be good," the voice on the other end said.

"We have a problem, sir," Tom replied. "A big problem."

"Where are we going?" Olivia asked when Billy pulled out of the parking lot and took a left instead of the right she'd expected.

"Your place."

She blinked. "My place? Why?"

"You need to pack some clothes for a few days."

She felt as if she'd just gotten whiplash. "I'm sorry?"

He glanced over at her, his expression tightly controlled. "It's not safe for you at home, Olivia. We have no evidence to back up Cooper's findings, he's missing, and we have no idea who's behind the cover up. It's better if you aren't easily found."

Her heart was beginning to slam into her ribs. Yes, she'd been scared last night, but it was daylight now and everything seemed a little less creepy than it had before. And yet she knew he was right. She couldn't stay in her apartment when she didn't know why Alan had sent her the disc, or where he was, or how they were going to get the evidence and stop the deal from going through.

"All right," she said carefully, "but I'll stay in a hotel."

"You'll stay with me."

"Billy—"

He flashed dark eyes at her. "Not negotiable, Livvie. You asked me to help you and the only way I can do that is if I know where you are at all times. You're staying with me, or I'm staying with you in that hotel. Your choice."

A small part of her cheered at the idea of being locked up with Billy Blake for the next few days. The rest of her was terrified.

"It's Christmas Eve. I don't want to ruin your plans."

"If that were true, you wouldn't have come to my house last night."

Her skin was on fire. She knew what he was implying. "If you're suggesting that I wanted to stop you from having a hot Christmas date, you're wrong. You're the only person I knew I could trust to help me figure this out. If you're sleeping with someone, I don't care."

"Didn't sound like that last night."

They drove alongside the Potomac, winding through the snowy city streets, and Olivia clutched her hands into fists and kept her gaze fixed on the scenery. "You took that wrong. I was curious, that's all. Same as you were."

"I wasn't curious. I was fucking jealous. And you know it."

A thrill shot through her to hear him say it. And longing. Such incredible longing. He didn't say anything else and they soon reached her apartment building. He went with her, up the elevator and down the hall to her door. She put the key in the lock nervously, knowing he was standing right behind her, and then the door swung open and she went inside.

He came in and shut the door, his gaze moving over the space, missing nothing.

"No tree?"

She shook her head. "I was too busy."

Plus she couldn't stand the sight of a tree in her own living room, knowing what she'd been doing last year on Christmas Eve. They'd slept on her couch, tangled in each other while Christmas carols played on the radio and the television blared *It's a Wonderful Life.*

Yes, it had been a wonderful life. Until she'd gotten scared. Until her fear of trusting anyone kicked in.

She turned to look at Billy and hoped she didn't look as emotionally battered as she felt. He stood there so tall and imposing in her space, his hands shoved into his pockets, his jaw tight. He was broad and beautiful and she wanted to go over and slip her arms around his waist just to bask in his heat and the security of his arms.

"Go," he said softly, as if he knew precisely what she was thinking. "Get packed so we can get out of here."

Olivia bit her lip as words of regret hovered on her tongue. But then she swallowed them down again and went to do as he told her.

SEVEN

BILLY BANGED AROUND IN THE kitchen, fixing dinner for him and Olivia. It was too uncomfortably like last year—and too uncomfortably not. She was here with him, but they weren't a couple. Not like last year. He had no right to strip her naked and take her every way he could think of until they fell into an exhausted sleep.

They hadn't been together long when Christmas rolled around last year, but everything about it had felt right with Olivia. He knew she didn't care for the holiday, and he knew why. He'd wanted to take her to Vermont and wrap her in his family's embrace for the season, but of course they hadn't had time for that. He'd thought maybe they would do it this year, but then their relationship ended and that was that.

He finished preparing the meatloaf, potatoes, and green beans and called her into the kitchen. She was so small and vulnerable as she walked in, buried under a giant sweatshirt and yoga pants with thick socks. Her blonde hair was tucked behind her ears and she looked more like a young girl than a public relations specialist for a defense contractor.

"Any word on Alan yet?" she asked, biting her lower lip in that gesture he knew meant she was worried. It also sent a curl of heat into his groin.

"Nothing. We're looking for him. We know he didn't leave the country, though. He didn't fly anywhere either, which means he isn't too far."

"He could have driven."

"He could have, but his credit cards haven't been used to buy gas. And he didn't withdraw a large amount of cash recently."

She shook her head. "I know I said it before, but it's amazing what you can find out about someone when you really want to know."

He turned back to the stove and fixed a plate for her. He could tell her how ridiculously easy it was to track someone you wanted to know about, but he didn't. For instance, he could tell her that as soon as he'd returned from the field that last time, when he'd expected her to be there for him, he'd figured out damn quick that she was in DC. And that she'd accepted a job with Titan Technology without telling him about it.

He'd known her address, her phone number, and precisely how long it would take to travel from Fort Bragg to her door. He'd stopped then, because if he'd kept finding out more, he might have lost his mind.

Instead, he'd done what he'd been doing since he was a kid and his mother dropped him off instead of keeping him. He coped. He got on with life. He didn't look back.

No time for regrets. No time for people who didn't want you.

"Thanks," she said when he handed her the plate. She

sat down at the table and speared some meatloaf. "God," she said after the first forkful, "I forgot how amazing you are in the kitchen."

He didn't say what he wanted to say, which was "And what about the bedroom? Did you forget that too? Do you need me to remind you?"

Instead, he fixed his own plate and joined her. She was looking down at the food instead of at him, her cheeks slashed with red, and he knew she'd connected *amazing* and *you* and *bedroom* in her own head. It should gratify him, but it didn't. It only made him crankier.

"We've been invited to Richie's house tomorrow."

She looked at him with something akin to panic in her expression. He'd used Matt Girard's team name, but she knew the team names. "I can't go."

"Why not?"

"Because I wasn't supposed to be here, that's why. And because it'll be awkward."

"Because we used to be a couple, you mean?"

She nodded.

"Evie's been planning this party for weeks and I said I'd be there. If I go, you go. And I'm going."

She set her fork down. "I know you're pissed at me, Billy. I can feel the anger rolling off you. For what it's worth, I'm sorry. But I really don't think I have a place at a team gathering. I don't even know this Evie person. Is that Matt's girlfriend? His mother?"

"His fiancée."

She looked a little surprised at that information. "I didn't know. Wow, he's getting married? While on the teams?"

"Why not? For some of the guys, it works just fine.

They don't need to choose one or the other."

Her face paled a little. "I suppose I deserve that."

She did, but it didn't make him feel any better.

"Jesus," he said. "Just eat, Livvie. Forget it."

Her green eyes were soft, a little sad. "I'm not sure either one of us is going to forget it. It's Christmas Eve, and we both know what the elephant in the room is."

He was looking at her with that hot gleam in his eyes that said he knew exactly what she was talking about. Of course he did. They both did. Sex hung in the air between them, surrounded them, and permeated everything they did together. It was a monumentally bad idea for her to be here, yet here she was. And she'd fought so hard against that idea, hadn't she?

Oh, she'd mentioned she should stay in a hotel, but she'd not really argued with him, had she? And there *had* been other solutions. She could have asked for one of the other guys to be her bodyguard, and then none of this chaotic emotion would be happening right now. She probably *should* have asked for one of the other guys.

But she hadn't. And though she didn't want to admit it to herself, she knew why she hadn't.

Because she'd missed Billy. Because being near him again was as intoxicating as it was infuriating. Because she felt more alive than she'd felt in months now that she was with him. And because it was Christmas and she didn't want to be with anyone else.

"Yeah, I guess we do," he said. "Last year was pretty spectacular, huh?"

"It definitely was."

He arched an eyebrow. "Nothing stopping us from doing it again. I'm game if you are."

Her heart lurched hard. She wanted to. She really did. But it was so much more complicated than that. If she undressed for him, she'd be baring more than her body. She'd be baring her heart. Because she hadn't stopped caring for him.

"It wouldn't be the same." What if it was just sex for him now? What if they made love all night long and then he said goodbye as soon as this was over?

If he told her he cared, even just a little bit; if he said it would be the same because the emotion was the same; if he stroked his fingers along her cheek and said it would be beautiful because she was beautiful, she'd melt into his arms right this minute.

He looked at her for a long moment. "Yeah, probably right. Why ruin a great memory?"

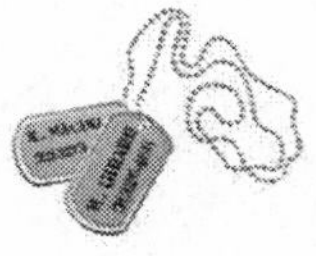

Olivia's cell phone rang in the middle of the night, waking her out of a deep sleep. She fumbled for it in the dark, but she missed the call. It went to voicemail and she pressed buttons, bleary-eyed as she tried to figure out who had called. It was probably her mother, but the number had a Virginia area code, so that couldn't be right. She hit redial and waited, but no one picked up.

There was a ding indicating she had voicemail. The recording was terrible, as if the person on the other end was in an area with bad reception. Or maybe someone had just butt-dialed her. It went on for a minute in which she couldn't make out anything. She almost erased it, but some little instinct told her not to do so.

She lay there for a few minutes, and then she got up and went to find Billy. If he was asleep, she wouldn't wake him, but if he was on the computer, she'd ask him to listen. The house was quiet, but there was a glow coming from the living room where he'd pitched his sleeping bag.

Except it wasn't a computer. She stopped in the door and stared at the tree. He'd plugged it in. The white lights glowed softly while a few small ornaments glinted. She put her hand to her mouth. He'd decorated the tree and lit it while she slept. Because that's what he did to honor his aunt. Because he had a family who celebrated Christmases and who loved each other deeply.

She'd never had that. She'd had a drunken mother and a succession of men who weren't her daddy. Darrel had tried, but even he'd given up when continually faced with the relentless wall of her mother's alcoholism.

"I can hear you breathing, Livvie," he said, and she started because she hadn't realized he was awake. He was lying in the bag, facing the tree, and she'd thought he was sleeping.

"I got a call," she said, only now realizing she'd walked out here in his T-shirt and socks again. Her nipples budded tight as she remembered the way he'd looked at her last night.

"I heard the phone ring." He turned over in the bag, one arm behind his head. "Was it important?"

"I don't know. I thought it was a butt-dial. But then I thought I should run it past you before I deleted it."

He sat up and she walked over, suddenly conscious of bare muscle and smooth skin rippling in the dim light of the tree. Her body bloomed with heat. It flooded her limbs, her belly, her sex. She was hot and aching and all she wanted was for Billy to reach out and touch her.

She handed him the phone, careful not to let her fingers brush his. He listened to the message and then checked out the number it came from.

"Don't recognize it?"

"No."

He shoved a hand through his hair and yawned. Then he reached for his laptop—of course it wasn't far away—and powered it up. A little bit of typing and then he looked up at her.

"It's a burner."

She knew what that meant. A disposable cell phone that people used when they didn't want to be traced.

"It could be Alan."

"It could be." He picked up his own phone and made a call. "Hey man, got something for you. Need you to analyze a recording."

He gave the person on the other end her number and then demanded her voicemail password. She hesitated, but then she gave it to him. If she didn't, he'd find a way to hack into it. Besides, he was trying to find Alan and stop Titan from selling faulty equipment to the Army. What did her privacy matter compared to that?

"If there's anything on there, we'll find it," he told

her once he finished the call.

"I know." There was a lump in her throat. She'd always known how critical his job was, but now that she was a part of what he was doing, it hit her just how important it was. And how good he was at it. From the minute she'd spilled the story, he'd been working to uncover the truth. He could have sent her away, but he hadn't. There was no proof that what Alan alleged was the truth, but Billy and HOT acted like it could be.

"You're thinking awful hard, Liv."

She tore her gaze from the tree and looked down at him. His brows were drawn low as he studied her.

"Everything all right?"

She swallowed. "Yes."

He sighed. "You want to talk about it?"

She wrapped her arms around her body and stood there, shivering. "I just want this to be over. I want Alan to be safe—and I want you to be safe."

Her voice broke at the end and he got to his feet, drawing her into his embrace. She wrapped her arms around him automatically and pressed her cheek to his bare chest.

"I am safe, Liv."

"Not if Titan sells that equipment to the Army."

His hand was on her hair, stroking her head. It felt so nice, so reassuring. "They won't. We'll make sure of it."

"All I ever wanted was for you to be safe, Billy." Her voice was hoarse with the effort to hold back tears of frustration and anger—with herself, with him, with this whole damn situation between them.

"I know."

She tilted her head back to gaze up into his face. He

was so handsome he took her breath away. His expression was fierce and controlled at once. And vulnerable in a way she hadn't expected. As if he feared her as much as she feared him.

"When I left..." She pulled in a breath. "I couldn't bear the thought of something happening to you out there. I panicked."

She'd thought it would be easier if she left on her own terms instead of risk her heart again and again.

"I know that too." He ran his hands over her shoulders and then he pushed her gently away from his body. "Something else I know is that unless you walk away right now, you're mine for the rest of the night."

EIGHT

OLIVIA COULDN'T BREATHE. SHE KNEW she should walk away, the same as she did last night, but she just couldn't seem to make her feet move. This was Billy Blake, the man she'd loved—hell, the man she still loved—and he was standing here in front of her with nothing but a pair of boxers on his gorgeous body. The Christmas lights illuminated his skin, delineating every bulge and curve of muscle.

Muscle she wanted to touch and lick and feel moving beneath her hands. She vibrated with need, her body liquefying beneath his hot gaze.

"Liv? You gotta go, babe. I can't take this much longer."

She swallowed. "I don't want to go."

It was his turn to swallow. "You better be sure about that."

She stepped into his arms again, ran her hands up the smooth skin of his back. "I'm sure." Terrified, but sure.

His mouth crushed down on hers then and she whimpered at the feel of his tongue sliding between her lips. It had been so long. Too long.

He kissed her hard and deep, and she met him as ravenously as he met her. Their tongues slid and tangled, their bodies pressing together, their hands gliding over skin and muscle. Billy reached for the hem of the T-shirt and ripped it up and over her head. Then he cupped her ass, groaning when he realized she wasn't wearing any panties.

He picked her up then and she wrapped her legs around his hips, still kissing him, her hands on either side of his face, holding him right where she wanted him. It felt so good to kiss him again, so damn good.

Her heart was ready to pound right out of her chest. And her body… God, her body was on fire. She could come just from kissing him if he kept this up. He was so damn hot, so perfect.

He finally broke the kiss and pressed his lips to her neck. And then he licked a path to her breasts, sucking a nipple into his mouth while she arched her back to give him better access. He was so big and strong, and he held her high while he licked her nipples over and over.

She was spread wide, her body open for him, so that it was no surprise when one of his fingers found the wet seam of her sex. When he reached her clitoris, she thought she would die. He flicked it lightly, expertly, while he sucked hard on her nipple and she clutched his shoulders, arching her hips, animal sounds coming from her throat.

"Billy," she gasped as he did it again. "Please."

"Please what, Liv? Please make you come? Please end this torture? Please fill you with my cock?"

"All of it. Please, all of it."

He took her down to the floor then, placing her on top of the sleeping bag and kissing her over and over while she melted beneath him. Her skin was on fire, her body so tight with anticipation that it hurt.

"Dammit, I want this to last," he said as she ran her hands down his sides and shoved at the waistband of his boxers. But he gave in to her efforts and kicked the shorts off. And then he was naked and she wrapped a hand around his cock while he groaned. "Livvie."

"I've missed you, Billy," she said, her throat thick with emotion. "So much."

Somehow she managed to push him onto his back, and then she straddled him and did all the things with her tongue that she'd been dying to do. She licked her way down the solid wall of his pectorals, over the ridges of his abdomen, until she could press his thick cock to her cheek and feel the heat of him.

But then she took him into her mouth, her tongue swirling over the velvety head, down the ridge in the center. He fisted his hands in her hair and she could feel him breathing hard and fast, trying so hard not to let go, not to come straight away.

She wouldn't mind if he did. It made her feel powerful to know she could still do this to him, that he was—for the moment anyway—submissive and vulnerable to her touch. She sucked him a little harder then and his back bowed.

"God, Olivia. When you do that—"

He didn't finish what he was saying, and she didn't care. She loved the feel of him in her mouth, the salty taste of his flesh, the sounds he made. Her body hurt with arousal, but there would be time enough for her later.

But he reached for her, urged her up until her knees were on either side of his head. Then he buried his tongue in the soft, wet heat of her—and Olivia came unglued.

Her body exploded in a rush of light and feeling, but Billy didn't stop. He kept licking her, sucking her, forcing her body toward another crisis. Somewhere, in the intensity of what he did to her, she tried to do the same to him. But her rhythm was knocked off balance now and all she could focus on was the pleasure coursing through her.

When she came again, his name on her lips, he flipped her over and sank down on top of her. He braced himself above her, his expression dark and intense as his gaze raked hers.

"Do I need a condom?"

She knew what he was asking. If she'd been with anyone else without one. If she was still on the pill. She shook her head and then he bent down slowly and took her mouth with his own.

He kissed her softly at first, his cock nudging into her slick heat. Olivia wrapped her legs around him and he sank down into her, stealing her breath away with his heat and size and the sheer pleasure of being impaled by him again.

The softness didn't last. Neither of them was capable of it, really. Not after so long. Billy hooked an arm around one of her legs and opened her wider, pounding into her harder and harder with each stroke.

The pleasure stretched and spiraled, growing tighter and tighter inside her belly, her sex, until she was ready to scream. He got onto his knees then, lifted her to him. And then he brought her legs tightly together and stroked into her until the friction caught at her G-spot and sent her careening over the edge of one of the best orgasms of her life.

He didn't give her time to recover. He urged her onto

all fours and plunged into her from behind. She didn't think she could come again, but she was wrong. His fingers set up a rhythm against her clitoris that matched the rhythm of his strokes—

And she shattered. This time, he went with her, his body jerking as he came deep inside her.

They collapsed to the floor together, breathing hard and trying to reconcile what had just happened with everything they'd believed up until this moment. Olivia felt hot tears spill down her cheeks. She turned her head into the sleeping bag and tried to hide but her body began to shake with the intensity of her emotions.

"Olivia," he said behind her, his mouth falling to her shoulder, his arm tightening around her waist. "Don't cry, baby. Don't cry."

"I'm not crying over you, Billy," she said, trying to convince herself as much as him. "I'm crying because that felt so damn good. I was wound up tight and you unwound me. That's all."

His mouth was still on her shoulder, so gentle, so sweet. "I know, Livvie."

"I should go," she said, though she didn't really want to. But if she stayed, she'd end up deeper in love with him than ever. And she still didn't know what the future held. If she could trust him to be there for her, or if he'd go away and get killed in a warzone. If he'd leave her.

He turned her in his arms then, came up on an elbow beside her and stroked the tears away with his fingers. "Stay with me."

The tree twinkled and she could see snow falling when she looked up at the window. Billy was beside her, warm and solid and alive, and something inside her twisted, like a key fitting into a lock. He was the key, she realized. The key to her heart.

And though it frightened her to let him in, even a little bit, she lifted her arms and put them around his neck. "Yes," she said simply. Because, for her, there was no other choice.

Billy couldn't take his eyes off Olivia. He watched her laughing with Evie, and with Sam McKnight's fiancée, Georgeanne Hayes. Liv was gorgeous, but it was more than that. There was something about this one woman that tore him up inside and made him willing to do anything to keep her happy.

Anything to keep her.

He hadn't expected to make love to her for half the night, but that's exactly what had happened. The best Christmas present ever in his opinion. If he were lucky, he'd take her home and do it all again tonight.

"Looks like you got it bad, Kid."

Billy jerked his head up to find Sam standing beside him. Sam's gaze strayed to the women and Billy wondered if the gleam in the man's eyes as he looked at his fiancée was anything like the way Billy looked at Olivia.

"Pot and kettle, dude," he said softly.

Sam laughed. "Yeah, no doubt."

Matt wandered over and joined them. "Y'all hungry? Evie's been at it since daybreak."

"Smells amazing," Billy said. He already knew it would be. Evie Baker couldn't cook a bad meal.

Matt took a sip of his drink. It looked like a mixed drink—cola and something—but Billy knew better. Richie Rich didn't drink. Ever.

"Got some news on that recording," Matt said, and Billy's gaze whipped to his commanding officer. "Nothing good, I'm afraid. It's a car radio in the background. The station was DC Metro."

"So whoever called Olivia was in a car and in the local area."

"Yeah."

Billy blew out a breath. "Not helpful at all."

Matt looked unhappy. "No. And nothing new on Titan either. Mendez is digging. He's called some of his contacts at the NSA. But there's nothing, other than a tenuous connection to Congressman Black. It's his district that will benefit the most if the deal goes through. That's not enough to stop it. We need hard evidence."

Sam said, "Congress hasn't voted yet. We have time."

"Not a lot, but yeah, we have time." Matt looked up as the women laughed, his gaze seeking Evie. He stood there for a long minute, about as lost in Evie as Sam and Billy had been in Georgie and Olivia. The only difference, Billy thought with envy, was that Sam and Matt knew where they were headed with their women.

"We need to find Cooper," Billy said. He wanted to get this over with and behind them so he could figure out what was going on with him and Olivia too. Could he let her back into his life again? Or was it best if they left it at a few nights of hot sex and moved on?

He knew she'd had a shitty childhood, and he knew

she didn't trust easily. He'd been pissed when she'd asked him to give up HOT, but he understood where it came from.

"If he's still alive," Jack Hunter said, and Billy started because Hawk had a way of being there and not being there at the same time. He'd been so damn quiet that Billy hadn't noticed him. But he was sitting on the couch, a beer in his hand, his surfer-boy looks as golden and gleaming as ever—except for a darkness in his blue eyes that said he wasn't the pretty boy everyone assumed he was on first glance. No, he definitely wasn't. When it was necessary, Hawk was a cold-blooded killing machine capable of taking out a target from over a mile away with his sniper rifle.

No one said anything for a long moment. The doorbell rang and Matt went to answer it. A few seconds later he came back with Kevin MacDonald and Lucky San Ramos in tow. Lucky looked stone-faced and Kev looked as if he could chew nails for breakfast. Man, Billy didn't envy Kev this detail at all. It was clear as hell that Kev was in love with Lucky—and that he was determined not to let it show.

As for Lucky, who knew? She didn't look happy, that was for sure. And why would she be when she was about to put her life on the line searching for the terrorist who'd tortured her?

Lucky went to join the other women while the men sat in the living room with the Christmas tree twinkling, carols playing softly, and the irritation of being unable to find Alan Cooper—or the evidence to blow the Titan deal out of the water—hanging over their heads like a malevolent cloud.

As the afternoon wore on, they tried to put the situation behind them as much as possible. The food was amazing, as always, and the camaraderie with these guys couldn't be beat. They were brothers, even if they weren't actually related. Billy would trust his life with any one of these guys, and they with him.

And they all had, many times.

Eventually, it was time to say goodbye. Billy helped Olivia into the truck and they drove the distance back to his house without saying much. There was an awkwardness between them, but there was also heat and want. No matter how desperately he wanted her again, he decided to let her be the one to make the first move. If she fled when they got back to his place, he'd respect that.

Except his cock was half-hard already, remembering the way she'd melted around him last night, her body opening to him, her soft cries of pleasure ringing in his ears. Billy shook his head. He needed to focus, needed to think about what else he could possibly do to find Cooper or discover who was behind the conspiracy.

He pulled into his driveway, still thinking about how he wanted to strip Olivia naked the instant they walked through the door. He'd just gotten out of the truck when it hit him that something didn't feel right.

Before he could figure out why that was, a gun jammed right up beneath his ribs. It wasn't anything he hadn't experienced before so he didn't panic. He just put up his hands and tried to assess the situation. He could disarm the guy easily, even now—

Except Olivia stumbled around the front of the truck then, her eyes wide with fear as another guy had one arm wrapped around her and a gun to her jaw.

"Do anything, anything at all," a menacing voice behind him said, “and Miss Reese will die.”

NINE

THEY WERE LOCKED IN A warehouse. Billy was zip-tied with his hands behind his back but they'd left Olivia free. It was almost an insult, but then she was thankful they hadn't thought her enough of a threat to tie her up.

The warehouse was empty, except for a couple of chairs and a table, so there wasn't even anything they could really use to break free.

"I'm sorry, Billy," she said again.

He'd shut down a long time ago, his expression carefully blank. It scared her that he didn't show any emotion. How did he do that?

"It's not your fault, Liv."

"It is. I didn't think about my car." When she'd slid off the road, the car automatically dialed BMW. They'd asked her if she was okay and she'd said yes. They'd asked if she needed assistance and she'd said no. Because she'd known she was close to Billy's house and she'd intended to walk the rest of the way rather than wait an hour in the car for a man to show up with a tow truck. She'd been too scared to wait.

"Even if you'd told me, I might not have considered that someone would use the tracking information to find you."

But he would have. She knew it as sure as she knew her own name. It's what he did.

"I appreciate you trying to spare my feelings, but we both know I'm the reason we're here."

"No, we're here because someone wants to defraud the U.S. Government and put soldiers in danger just so they can make a quick buck."

He was pacing back and forth, his gaze flashing hot. Even with his arms behind him, he looked dangerous.

"Whoever this is, they have access, Liv. Your average guy isn't going to be able to use your BMW's tracking info to find you."

"You could," she said.

He gave her a grin that surprised her. "And who said I was average, babe?"

She sank down on one of the chairs and tried not to hyperventilate. Her heart was pounding hard. She wasn't accustomed to someone jamming a gun in her face and forcing her into a car. She'd been thinking about what was going to happen when the door closed to Billy's house, if she'd jump on him and strip him or try to remain cool, when someone grabbed her from behind and slapped a gloved hand over her mouth. She couldn't even warn Billy.

When the man had pushed her around the truck, she'd been relieved that Billy was still alive. And scared to death because she could see the violence in his eyes. He hadn't acted on it, however. He'd stayed cool, even when the men had marched them down the road to a waiting car and shoved them in it. If it had only been light out, they might have seen the guys waiting in ambush.

But they hadn't.

The door opened then and a man came in. Olivia was on her feet in a second.

"Tom! What the hell is going on?"

Tom Howard sauntered over with his hands in his pockets, looking apologetic. "I'm so sorry to put you through this. I'm afraid Alan has lost his mind." He waved a hand as if he were waving away a fly. "I tried to keep it quiet, but then he disappeared. He's dangerous, Olivia. Very dangerous."

Billy had leaned a hip against the table. He looked so casual, as if they were still at Matt and Evie's place and he was just listening to the conversation.

"I'm sorry to hear that," Olivia said, focusing on Tom again. "But I don't know how I can help."

"He sent you something. I'd like to see it."

"I don't have it." Which was true. She'd turned the disc over to HOT yesterday in case they could find some sort of DNA evidence on it that might help.

Tom's forehead was shiny. He smiled again. "What did you do with it?"

She shrugged. Maybe she should have denied that Alan had sent her anything, but then she knew that the best lies were those closest to the truth.

"There was nothing really on it. Just some notes of Alan's." She forced a laugh. "He tried to say the test results were wrong, but there was no evidence of it. I think he probably wanted to give the company a black eye."

Tom's eyes gleamed. "But what did you do with the disc?"

"I shredded it."

Tom stared at her for a minute. And then he tsked. "Olivia, why are you lying to me? You brought this man—" he jerked his head at Billy "—to the office yesterday. Why would you do that if you weren't looking for something?"

Olivia's pulse thrummed. She didn't dare look at Billy. "Sex," she said softly. "He's pretty hot and I..." She swallowed. "I wanted to impress him so he'd sleep with me."

"Jesus, Tom," someone said from the door. "The girl's lying. Shoot the bastard and then she'll tell you what you want to know."

Another man came into the light then. He was tall and wore a long cashmere coat. His hair was brown with just a hint of gray on the sides. He was elegant and cultured—and recognizable. But she couldn't worry about Congressman Black at the moment. Instead, her attention was focused on the man walking behind him. The one who held up a gun and pointed it at Billy's heart.

"Go ahead," Black said, shrugging.

"No," Olivia cried, rushing toward the man with the gun. The gun swung at her and she crashed to a stop. It's what she'd wanted, but having a gun pointed at her wasn't any better. "I didn't shred it. I gave it to an elite Special Operations unit."

Congressman Black swore. Tom paled. The man with the gun didn't move. Black stood there for a long moment. And then he shrugged.

"There's nothing to connect me to it, Tom," he said. "And I intend to keep it that way." He jerked his head at the armed guy. "Need it to look like an accident. A murder-suicide."

"And Howard?"

Black considered it for a long moment. "Suicide is the only honorable way out."

They were alone again, waiting while the men outside this room figured out precisely how to deal with them. They'd taken Tom with them, but Olivia couldn't spare a thought for him. All she could think about was Billy and everything she wished she'd ever said or done.

"I didn't expect it to end like this," she said.

"It's not over, Livvie. Don't give up."

"I know you're trained to get out of bad situations, but you usually have your team behind you. Or a weapon at least. All you've got is a couple of chairs, a table, and me. And you're tied up. I don't see how this can work in our favor."

"Faith, babe. Have some faith."

She sat on one of the chairs and looked up at him standing there, so vibrant and strong. He was a warrior and he wasn't giving up. But she felt like she had when she'd been a kid and her mother waltzed in and informed her they were moving again. Whichever boyfriend she'd had at the time had either walked out or kicked her out and it was time to go. Olivia had fought at first, but she'd learned to face her fate stoically over the years. It was adapt or go crazy.

But this wasn't the kind of fate you accepted without a fight, was it? Hell no.

"Tell me what to do, Billy. I'll be ready."

"Just stay out of the way, Liv. That's all you need to do."

Her eyes filled with tears. "Don't get yourself killed, okay?"

He came over and bent down to kiss her. Their mouths met urgently, tongues tangling, regret and passion mingling.

"I love you," she said when he broke the kiss, her hand sliding along his jaw. She wanted to touch him everywhere, wanted to lose herself in him.

He grinned at her and she wondered how he could be so jovial. "I love you too, Liv."

Her heart squeezed tight. She felt such joy—and such crushing sorrow that this was the end.

"I should have trusted you, Billy. I should have stayed."

"Yeah, you should have. But you can spend the rest of your life making it up to me."

She tried not to laugh. "All fifteen minutes or so of it?"

"Longer than that, Liv. Way longer. I need to make you pay for leaving me."

Her emotions were getting the better of her now. "I'm sorry I asked you to leave HOT."

"I would have done it for you."

She shook her head. "You don't have to say that."

"I know, but I mean it. I was coming home to tell you after that last mission. I'd work a desk for you, if that's what it took to make you happy."

She stood and wrapped her arms around him. "You make me happy. Just you."

He kissed her and she melded herself to him, desperate for one last happy moment with him. There was a rattling at the door and she whimpered.

"Need to go to work now, babe. Step back and stay back."

"Billy, please," she said. "Please."

His dark eyes sparked. "It's okay, Liv. Trust me."

She took a step back. The door was sliding open then. Billy leaned forward and slammed his bound hands up and then down hard, against his back. He did it again just as two men walked into the room. They were both armed.

Suddenly, Billy was in motion. He moved so fast she couldn't quite tell what he did, but there was the sound of fists and feet hitting flesh—and then the two guys were on the ground and Billy stood over them with two guns pointed at two heads.

Olivia realized that her hand was over her mouth. She let it drop slowly, her eyes wide. He'd gotten free. And he'd taken out two gunmen.

"You could have done that at any time," she said in wonder.

He didn't make eye contact. "Yeah, but I did it when it was most useful."

"But how? You were tied so tight."

"Zip ties are easy as hell to break out of if you know what you're doing. You hear that, assholes?" he said to the men on the floor. "Easy."

He motioned her over. "Now get behind me and stay there."

She did as he told her and they moved through the

door. He paused to slide it shut and lock it and then they were moving down a dark corridor and all she could hear was the sound of her breath and thumping pulse. Billy was stealthy, but she felt like an elephant moving along behind him.

He stopped to listen and she fisted her hands in his jacket and waited. And then a door opened to her left. Billy was spinning toward the sound, trying to shove her behind him, when someone grabbed her and a gun jammed up into her jaw. She couldn't see the man but she could smell his cologne. And feel the soft cashmere of his coat.

"I have nothing to lose," Congressman Black said. "But you do. Drop the weapon or I'll kill her."

Billy's jaw was hard, his eyes glittering hot and furious. She knew he could save himself, knew he could take this man out—but the risk was her, and she knew he wouldn't do it. He would drop the weapons and wait for another chance.

And if she knew anything at all about the man holding her so tight right now, she knew he wasn't going to allow Billy another chance to do anything. The instant his hand lowered, the Congressman would drop him where he stood.

Olivia wasn't about to let that happen. She hadn't been in the Special Forces, but she'd been in the Army and she had combat training. She sucked in a breath and brought her elbow back as hard as she could at the same time she brought her foot down on the Congressman's instep.

Everything seemed to happen in slow motion then. Olivia's elbow and foot connected, Billy yelled and lunged, and the Congressman's arm jerked. There was a loud bang—or maybe it was two—the smell of spent gunpowder, and a ringing in her ears.

Billy had her in his arms then. His mouth was moving but she couldn't hear him. She smiled up at him and lifted her hand to touch his face. He jerked her off her feet and then he was running, running, running through the dark corridors—

He burst outside into the cold air and men appeared from all directions, dressed in dark clothes, wearing headsets and carrying weapons.

Badasses. Those HOT boys were such badasses.

That was the last thing she thought before she slipped away.

TEN

"IF YOU EVER DO THAT again, Olivia Reese, I'm spanking you in front of God and the world."

Olivia opened her eyes to find Billy hovering over her. She was lying flat on her back in a communications van. Above her, screens flickered with different angles of the warehouse they'd come out of.

"What happened?"

"You scared the shit out of me, that's what."

"Did I get shot?"

He shuddered. "No. But that gun went off so close to your head—" He clenched his jaw tight. "Another inch, Olivia."

"I couldn't let him shoot you."

He bent over her then and fused his mouth to hers. She sighed and put her arms around his neck. But then he pulled away again. "I wasn't going to let him shoot me. I told you I had it under control."

"You were going to drop the gun, Billy. And he would have shot you when you did."

His voice was hard. "I wasn't going to drop it. I was

going to drop *him*."

"While he had a gun to my head?"

"I wouldn't have missed, babe."

Olivia shivered, both from the cold and from how lethal this man was when he had to be. She'd known the military fighting machine was inside there, but she'd never seen it in action before. "So I guess I passed out, huh?"

"Shock."

She pushed herself up until she was sitting. She was embarrassed and relieved all at once. "My heart was beating so hard. I'm surprised I didn't pass out sooner."

"You did really good, Liv."

She reached for his hand and threaded her fingers in his. "So what happens now?"

"We wait for HOT to clean up."

She remembered that swarm of black-clad men right before she'd passed out. "How did they know where to find us?"

He looked a touch sheepish. "Tracking devices. I put one in your coat, one in mine. Just in case."

She blinked. "You thought we might get grabbed?"

"No, but I believe in being prepared. When I didn't answer my phone at check-in, the guys pulled us up on satellite."

"Wow," she said softly. "You really do think of everything."

"It's my job."

Olivia pulled her knees up and put her arms around them. "I can't believe Congressman Black was involved." It occurred to her then that she'd heard two shots instead of one. "Did you kill him?"

"No. But he might be missing a few fingers."

"What about Tom? And Alan?"

Billy let out a long breath and she knew the news wasn't going to be good. "The police found Alan Cooper a couple of hours ago. His car was parked in a townhouse garage over in McLean. The radio was on and the phone he called you from was with him. The battery was drained."

"Is he dead?"

"Yes. A neighbor noticed the smoke coming from under the garage and called the police. It was too late to save him by then."

Her eyes filled with tears. She hadn't known Alan well, but he'd seemed nice enough. On the other hand, he'd known about the technology and he'd waited to do anything about it.

Even then, he hadn't come forward himself. He'd involved her when all he'd needed to do was call the Pentagon.

"Did he kill himself?"

"I know it might make it easier if he had, but no. Someone knocked him over the head and put him there. He must have come to just long enough to try and phone someone. It's also possible he fell against the phone and it dialed you by accident."

Olivia shivered. "God, that's awful. What about the files? Was there anything there? Anything to stop the deal?"

"The Pentagon confiscated his computers. If it's there, we'll find it."

Had they gone through all this for nothing? It made her furious to think so. "What about Congress and the vote?"

"After tonight, Titan Technology won't be selling anything to the Pentagon. The lead engineer is dead. Tom Howard's going to jail, and the Congressman will be joining him. No one's going to vote to approve a technology associated with a scandal like this one. And don't forget we still have Alan's notes. Those tests will be duplicated. If the results are what he said they were, everyone will know it."

Olivia let out the breath she'd been holding. "I knew it was a good idea to come to you for help."

He reached out and ran his fingers over her jaw while her skin tingled in response.

"You can always count on me, Livvie."

The Christmas tree sparkled in the night, its white lights painting the living room in a soft glow. Outside, the snow was coming down again, but in the house the occupants were tangled together inside a sleeping bag on the floor.

It was still Christmas, but barely. Another fifteen minutes and it would be midnight. Billy rolled Olivia beneath him and sank into her body while she arched up to him and kissed him. This was home. Right here with her, beneath the tree, deep inside her, his body on fire with longing and lust and love.

"I love you," she said as he thrust into her and she convulsed around him, her inner muscles squeezing him tight as she fell over the edge.

He loved it when she came, when her head went back and her throat arched up and her breath caught and then spilled in those soft sounds of pleasure that he adored.

He nipped her throat, sucked a nipple into his mouth and tugged just enough to make her cry out again.

"Billy, oh Billy…"

And then he slid into her again and again, harder and faster, until he reached his own peak, until his eyes closed and his head went back and he lost all sense of time and place. It felt so damn good with her. So right.

He collapsed beside her and drew her in close, curling around her from behind. "I love you, Olivia. Everything about you. I have from almost the first moment we met."

She turned in his arms then, until she was looking up at him with wide green eyes. He could see the sheen of tears in them. "You don't have to say that."

"I know I don't have to. But from the first time we made love, I knew it was different with you."

Her lashes dropped down over her eyes. "I nearly ruined it, didn't I? Demanding you quit HOT, disappearing while you were out in the field." She sighed then. "I'm almost as crazy as my mother."

He tipped her chin up. "You aren't crazy. And we're here together, aren't we? That's all that matters. We're together. It's Christmas. And I'm not letting you go again. If you walk out, I'm coming after you."

She laughed. "And I know you could find me no matter where I went."

"Damn right."

She spread her palms over his chest. "It was rotten of me to leave you like that, knowing what your mother did."

His heart pinched. “Your mother taught you that men couldn’t be relied on. Mine taught me that people who’re supposed to love you the most leave you. But we aren’t them. We make our own choices, Olivia. And I choose to be with you.”

Her mouth turned down in a little frown. “I don’t want you to leave HOT. Not unless it’s something you decide to do because you want to. Don’t ever give it up for me.”

“Marry me, Livvie.”

Her eyes grew wide. Her pink lips fell open. She gaped like a fish. “Are you serious?”

He snorted. “I’m naked in a sleeping bag under a Christmas tree with you and I’ve just told you that I’ve loved you from the first. Would I ask you if I wasn’t serious?”

“You didn’t ask, actually. You kind of stated it.”

She was biting her lip and he knew she was trying not to smile. “Hell yeah I stated it. I don’t want to give you a chance to say no.”

“I won’t say no,” she whispered.

His heart stopped beating. And then it lurched forward again and he let out a whoop before fusing his mouth to hers.

“This is the best Christmas ever,” Olivia said some time later. “The best present ever.”

“Copy that,” Billy said, skimming his hands over her naked body. “You are one hot package, Olivia Reese.”

She laughed. “And here I was thinking you were the one with the hot package.”

“Mmm,” he said nuzzling her throat. “Maybe I am. Want a demonstration?”

She arched her body against him. "Oh yes. Definitely. As often as possible."

"You got it, babe. For the rest of our lives."

ABOUT THE AUTHOR

USA Today bestselling author Lynn Raye Harris lives in Alabama with her handsome former-military husband and two crazy cats. Lynn has written nearly twenty novels for Harlequin and been nominated for several awards, including the Romance Writers of America's Golden Heart award and the National Readers Choice award. Lynn loves hearing from her readers.

Connect with Lynn online:
Facebook: www.facebook.com/AuthorLynnRayeHarris
Twitter: twitter.com/LynnRayeHarris
Website: www.LynnRayeHarris.com
Newsletter: http://eepurl.com/c5QFY

Made in the USA
Middletown, DE
29 February 2016